This book is given with love

TO:

_____

FROM:

_____

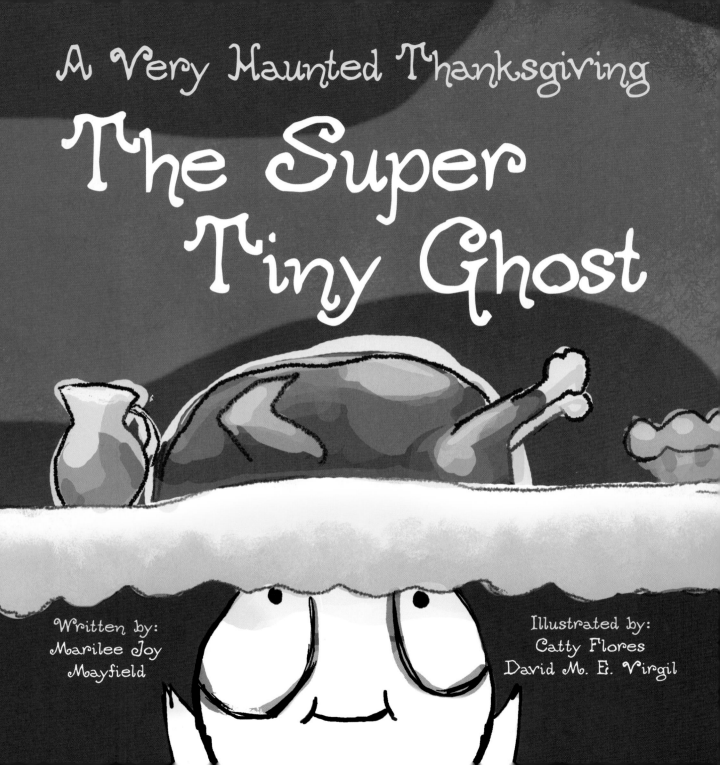

A Very Haunted Thanksgiving

The Super Tiny Ghost

Written by:
Marilee Joy
Mayfield

Illustrated by:
Catty Flores
David M. E. Virgil

Life wasn't easy

for the super tiny ghost,

He flew in and out of homes

all along the coast.

But when someone found out

where he had been haunting,

They chased him away

with their shouts and their taunting.

Soon there were no homes
to haunt anymore,
So he traveled along
the edge of the shore.
There he spied
a small fishing boat,
And above the waves
he began to float.

When he got there
he made himself at home,
There were lots of new places
for him to roam.
He even made friends
with the fisherman's cat,
And pretended he was captain
where the old man sat.

But the grouchy, old sailor
didn't want to house a ghost,
Even one that was tiny
and moaned less than most.
So he blew the foghorn
so suddenly and loud,
That the ghost zoomed away
like a tiny, frightened cloud.

For a while he drifted
on the sandy beach,
A home of his own
seemed far out of reach.
But then, just as he planned
to give up his dream,
Something made him perk up
with an excited scream!

It was an abandoned house
at the top of a hill,
The windows were broken,
and leaves entered at will.
There were cobwebs and spiders
and bats in the attic,
When the little ghost found it,
he was ecstatic!

It was the perfect place
for a ghost to live,
The steps squeaked loudly
and the floors had give.
The wind shrieked at night
in the glow of the moon,
And the super tiny ghost
used every room.

But after a time
he got lonely being there,
The portraits would just
gather dust and stare.
It was boring to be
by yourself every day,
With no one to scare
and no way to play.

The house was for sale,

but people just drove by...

No one wanted to give

this spooky house a try.

It looked haunted for sure

and was in need of repair;

The real estate agents

had given up in despair.

Once, an old lady came by
to take a look at the place,
And the little ghost whispered
a soft "hello" near her face.
She threw down her cane
and ran right out the door.
After that, no visitors
came by anymore.

The tiny ghost was alone,

until one blustery day,

When something unusual

came up the driveway.

The leaves were changing color

and it was a cold night,

When a car drove up,

an unexpected sight.

He looked out the window
from the top floor,
When a strong gust of wind
blew open the door.
He thought for sure
the people would drive away,
He had given up hope
that anyone would stay.

But the car doors opened
and a family hopped out,
The mom and dad talked
as the children ran about.
When they walked in the door
the little ghost was quiet,
He thought about speaking
but decided not to try it.

As they glanced around
they saw much work to do,
The sounds were quite spooky
as the cold wind blew through.
The black bats were flapping
their wings near the ceiling,
There were tons of cobwebs
and all the paint was peeling.

"I think this house is haunted,"
said the mom, "...isn't it cool?"
The young boy nodded,
"Wait until I tell the kids at school!"
"You're right," said the dad,
"This is where we should stay!"
Only the little girl was quiet,
she didn't know what to say.

She walked up the stairs
and saw the ghost floating away,
"Come back," she said,
"I just want to play."
Suddenly, the super tiny ghost
felt tongue-tied and shy,
He was a little bit scared
but he didn't know why.

Soon they moved in
and started repairs,
But he noticed they left
the squeak in the stairs.
In fact, they seemed to discover
all his favorite places,
And left him to haunt
those still-ghostly spaces.

November was passing fast,

soon it was Thanksgiving Day.

They cleaned the whole house,

and their chores felt like play.

The children helped their mom

prepare different foods to try...

Turkey with stuffing,

cranberries, and pumpkin pie!

Then they sat down together
and as they started their meal,
Their dad stood up and said,
"Here's how I feel...
I'm so grateful and blessed
to be here with all of you,
In our wonderful home,
it's a dream come true!"

As they each expressed gratitude
for the previous year,
The super tiny ghost
shed a tiny, happy tear.
He had his own family now,
his presence was known.
In his home by the sea
he would never be alone.

🐾 Claim Your FREE Gift!

Visit ➤ PDICBooks.com/STGThanks

Thank you for purchasing The Super Tiny Ghost: A Very Haunted Thanksgiving, and welcome to the Puppy Dogs & Ice Cream family.

We're certain you're going to love the little gift we've prepared for you at the website above.